WALLACE AND GRACE

Take the Case

Agnes and Clarabelle

Agnes and Clarabelle Celebrate!

Stinky Spike the Pirate Dog

Stinky Spike and the Royal Rescue

Wallace and Grace Take the Case

Wallace and Grace and the Cupcake Caper

The Adventures of Caveboy

Caveboy Is Bored!

WALLACE AND GRACE
Take the Case

Heather Alexander

illustrated by **Laura Zarrin**

BLOOMSBURY
NEW YORK LONDON OXFORD NEW DELHI SYDNEY

To SL, for all the mysteries we've solved (and plotted) together —H. A.

To my husband, Iraj, for always being by my side —L. Z.

First published in the United States of America in May 2017
by Bloomsbury Children's Books
www.bloomsbury.com

Library of Congress Cataloging-in-Publication Data
Names: Alexander, Heather, author. | Zarrin, Laura, illustrator.
Title: Wallace and Grace take the case / by Heather Alexander ; illustrated by Laura Zarrin.
Description: New York : Bloomsbury, 2017. | Summary: Owl detectives Wallace and Grace solve the mystery of the spooky garden.
Identifiers: LCCN 2015023963
ISBN 978-1-61963-988-1 (hardcover)
ISBN 978-1-68119-080-8 (e-book) • ISBN 978-1-68119-081-5 (e-PDF)
Subjects: | CYAC: Mystery and detective stories. | Owls—Fiction. | Friendship—Fiction. | BISAC: JUVENILE FICTION / Readers / Chapter Books. | JUVENILE FICTION / Mysteries & Detective Stories. | JUVENILE FICTION / Animals / Birds.
Classification: LCC PZ7.A37717 Wal 2017 | DDC [Fic]—dc23
LC record available at https://lccn.loc.gov/2015023963

Art created with Blackwing pencils and Photoshop
Typeset in Burbank, Century Schoolbook, and Roger • Book design by John Candell
Printed in China by C&C Offset Printing Co., Ltd., Shenzhen, Guangdong
1 3 5 7 9 10 8 6 4 2

Table of Contents

Night Owl
Detective
Agency

CHAPTER 1
Hide-and-Seek

"The sun is going down!" called Grace. "It's time to get up!"

Wallace peered out from their home in the Old Tree. "It is too early," he said. He rubbed the sleep from his eyes. "The sky is not dark yet."

He pointed to their sign: NIGHT OWL DETECTIVE AGENCY. "We work at *night*," he reminded her.

"But I want to go, go, go!" said Grace. She flapped her wings. Grace was full of energy.

"Owls sleep in the day and go out at night," said Wallace. Wallace liked to follow the rules.

"I am making new rules," said Grace. "My first new rule is: Never wait for fun!" She handed him

sunglasses. “Put these on. Pretend it is night.”

“Okay,” said Wallace. When Grace wanted to go, she made Wallace go, too. He liked that about her.

Wallace and Grace were best friends. They were also partners in the Night Owl Detective Agency. They searched for clues together. Then they solved mysteries.

Wallace and Grace always found out whooo-done-it!

"What now? We have no case to solve," said Wallace. He liked having a case. He was a good detective. "Days without mystery are boring."

"I refuse to do boring," said Grace. "Let's play hide-and-seek."

"Great idea!" cried Wallace. Grace always found fun things to do. He liked that best about her.

They flew up over the trees. They flew to a yard near the Great Woods. Three white bedsheets dried on a line.

"You look for me first!" said Grace. She hid behind a sheet.

Wallace found her.

Then Wallace hid behind a sheet.

Grace found him.

“Let’s play one more time,” said Wallace. He spotted a black-and-white cat near a soccer ball. That gave him a great idea!

His feathers were brown. The tree trunks were brown. He hid in the trees. Now he was hard to find.

Grace looked inside a blue jay's nest. No Wallace.

She looked inside a big flowerpot. No Wallace.

She looked inside a garbage

can. *Pee-ew!* And no Wallace.

A good detective finds things, Grace thought. *Why can't I find a big brown owl?*

Grace looked and looked. The sky turned dark. The stars sparkled as bright as her shiny necklace. *If Wallace sparkled like I always do,* Grace thought, *finding him would be so much easier!*

But Wallace wasn't about glitter and glam. He was about dirt and earthworms and hiding.

"Wallace, where are you?" cried Grace.

Wallace did not answer. He liked hiding almost as much as he liked being a detective.

"Show yourself!" demanded Grace.

"Here I am, Grace," said Wallace. He popped out from behind a tree.

Grace laughed. "The tree trunk was a great hiding place. You blended right in!"

"Help!" called a voice.

Wallace took off his sunglasses. "Whooo said *help*?"

"I did!" called the same voice.

Wallace and Grace looked down. Edgar hopped in the tall grass.

"Help! I need detectives," called Edgar.

"That's us! We're detectives! Let's go!" said Grace.

"Eeeyoy!" cried Wallace. He was excited. A case to solve!

Wallace and Grace flew down to Edgar.

"What's wrong?" Grace asked the rabbit. "Why do you need help?"

"There is a ghost in the garden!" cried Edgar.

CHAPTER 2

Do They Take the Case?

"A ghost in the garden!" cried Grace. Her big eyes opened wide.

"Will you help me?" asked Edgar. His whiskers twitched. He looked scared.

"You want us to find the *ghost*?" asked Grace.

"The Night Owl Detective Agency is good at finding things," said Wallace. "But we have never found a ghost."

"I don't want you to *find* the ghost," said Edgar.

"What do you want us to do?" asked Grace.

"I want you to make the ghost *go away*," said Edgar. "Can you do that?"

"*Hmmm*," said Wallace. Wallace

always said *Hmmm* when he was thinking. Wallace did a lot of thinking.

He pulled out his detective notebook and his pencil. He had found the little pencil at a mini-golf

place. He had also found a yellow golf ball. He was good at spotting things from high in the sky.

Now he wrote in his notebook:

Ghost in garden.

"When did you see the ghost?" Grace asked Edgar.

Grace always asked the questions. Wallace wrote the answers. That was how they worked.

"Just now," said Edgar. "I was

munching leafy green kale in the garden. Then I saw something white."

White, wrote Wallace.

"Ghosts are white," said Grace.

"But so are baseballs. And marshmallows," said Wallace.

"It wasn't a marshmallow," said Edgar.

"Did you know that the

biggest marshmallow was taller than a house?" asked Grace. "It is a fact."

"Grace is full of facts," said Wallace.

"It was *not* a marshmallow," said Edgar. "Anyway, I am not scared of marshmallows!"

"A big marshmallow could be scary. Just saying," said Wallace. He liked to point out these things.

"Okay, fine. No marshmallow in

the garden," said Grace. "What did the white thing look like?"

"The white thing was floating," said Edgar.

Floating, wrote Wallace.

"Ghosts float!" cried Grace. "It was white, and it was floating. It *is* a ghost!"

"Hold up," said Wallace. "We need more facts."

"The white, floating thing made a noise," said Edgar. "A spooky noise."

"Ghosts make spooky noises," Grace said to Wallace.

"*Hmmm*," said Wallace. Then he wrote: Spooky noise.

"You need to stay away from that garden," Grace warned Edgar.

"I can't stay away! The kale in the garden is the best!" Edgar licked his lips. "But I don't want to share with a ghost. Will you take my case?"

Wallace and Grace looked at each other. The Night Owl Detective

Agency had rules. Rule #1 was: Both partners had to say yes.

They needed a Partner Talk.

"We will be back," Wallace told Edgar. Then he and Grace flew to a tree stump nearby.

Wallace quickly spotted a big beetle with a hard shell. He ate it with a big cruunnch.

Grace sighed. She wished she had seen that beetle first. Wallace was so good at finding things.

"Do you want to find a ghost?" Grace asked Wallace.

"We don't know that it *is* a ghost," said Wallace.

"It sounds like a ghost," said Grace. She pointed to his notes:

"Are you scared of a ghost?" asked Wallace.

"A little," said Grace. But Grace

was more than a little scared. She was *a lot* scared.

"Me, too," said Wallace.

"This is quite the quandary," said Grace.

"What does that mean?" asked Wallace. Grace liked to use big words.

"It means it is a tricky choice," said Grace.

"You could have just said that," said Wallace.

"I did." Grace folded her wings. "What should we do?"

"Edgar needs our help," said Wallace. "And detectives always help when they are needed."

"That is true," said Grace.

"Detectives are brave. We are detectives. I think we should be brave," said Wallace.

Grace gulped. This case was getting trickier and trickier!

"Okay. We will be brave," she said.

They flew back to Edgar.

"Wallace and Grace will take the case!" said Grace.

“Whoo-hoo!” Edgar hopped up and down.

“Let’s go find the ghost!” said Wallace.

CHAPTER 3

Who Is in the Garden?

"Wings in the air! Eyes on the ground!" said Wallace. "Follow me!"

He flew off to the garden. The garden had a tall fence to keep critters out, but Wallace flew over the fence. Grace flew over the fence. Edgar crawled under the

fence. The fence was not very good at keeping critters out!

"I saw the ghost over there." Edgar pointed to a big bush with pink flowers.

Wallace looked closely at the bush. “Do you see what I see?” he asked Grace.

“I sure do,” said Grace. She had super-good owl eyesight.

"Do you see the ghost?" asked Edgar. His rabbit eyes weren't so good.

"No. We see paw prints in the dirt," said Grace. "And that is a clue."

Paw prints, wrote Wallace in his notebook.

"Show us your foot, Edgar," said Grace.

Edgar lifted one foot. He wobbled to the left. He wobbled to the right. Standing on one foot was tricky!

Wallace and Grace looked at his paw.

"Edgar's paw is not the same as these paw prints in the dirt," said Grace. "Edgar's paw is bigger."

"That means that Edgar did not make these paw prints," said Wallace. "Someone with small feet was in the garden, too."

"It was the *ghost*!" cried Edgar.

"Hold up," said Wallace. "You saw a floating ghost. Right?"

"Yes," said Edgar.

"A *floating* ghost would not leave footprints,"

said Wallace. “Floating means flying, not walking.”

“Aha!” cried Grace. She felt less scared now. “And these prints look like animal paw prints.”

“But what about the white floating thing?” asked Edgar.

"Hmmm," said Wallace.

"We need to investigate," Grace told Edgar. "That's a big word for *look around.*"

Wallace stepped closer to the bush.

"Eeeyoy!" he cried. "Look!"

White fabric poked out from under the bush.

Then Wallace twisted his head almost all the way around. Owls can do that!

“Do you see what I see?” Wallace pointed at the yard.

Grace twisted her head around, too. “I do!” Grace grinned.

Edgar tried to twist his head

around. *Oww!* Rabbit heads don't do that!

"No fair!" cried Edgar. He stamped his foot. "I do not see what you see."

"Look at the bedsheets on the line," said Wallace.

"Do you see the empty clothespins?" asked Grace.

"Yes," said Edgar. He scratched his ear. "What does that mean?"

"The empty clothespins mean that one sheet is missing," said Grace. "There were three sheets when we were playing hide-and-seek. Now there are only two sheets."

"The missing sheet floated under this bush," said Wallace.

"Edgar, you saw a white

bedsheet floating. Not a ghost!" cried Grace. "Case closed."

Shake, shake, flap, flap. Grace did a celebration dance. They had solved the case!

"Excuse me." Edgar held up his paw to stop the celebration. "Bedsheets do *not* make spooky noises, and I heard spooky noises."

"The rabbit is right," said Wallace.

Grace stopped dancing.

"We forgot about the Night Owl Detective Agency Rule #2," said Wallace.

"What's that?" asked Edgar.

"Rule #2 is: The case is not over until everything makes sense," said Grace.

"A bedsheet making spooky noises does not make sense," said Wallace.

"Case *not* closed," said Grace. "We need to investigate more."

Wallace followed the paw prints around the bush to the fence. “Look at this,” he said. The dirt by the fence was all dug up.

“A sheet would float *over* the fence,” said Grace.

"Something crawled *under* the fence right by this bush," said Wallace.

"It wasn't me. I came in there." Edgar pointed to the other side of the garden.

"We need to see what is *under* the bush," said Wallace.

They stared at the bush for a long time. Was the ghost hiding under there?

"You first," said Grace.

"No. You first," said Wallace.

"Someone do something. I'm hungry," said Edgar.

"Fine. I will be courageous," said Grace. *Courageous* was a big word for *brave*.

"Are you sure?" asked Wallace.

Grace was not sure, but she stepped toward the bush anyway.

Thump! Thump! Grace's heart beat loudly. She took another step. Then another.

She bent down near the leaves. What would she find?

And then they heard it. The spooky noise!

Mew! Mew! Mew!

Grace tumbled back in fear.

“Oh no! The ghost!” cried Edgar. He began to hop away.

“Hold up,” said Wallace. “That doesn’t sound like a spooky ghost.”

Grace listened again.

"Mew! Mew! Mew!"

Then she looked down at the tiny paw prints. The prints matched the noise.

"I know who is in the garden!" said Grace. "Do you?"

CHAPTER 4
Found!

"Yes, I know who is in the garden," said Wallace. "And it is not a ghost." He had solved the mystery at the same time as Grace. They were good partners that way.

"Who is it?" asked Edgar.

"We will show you," said Grace. "Ready?"

Wallace nodded. He pushed back the bush with his wing.

"Mew! Mew! Mew!"

"Kittens!" cried Edgar. Three kittens sat on a white sheet. "How did they get here?"

“We saw Mother Cat in the yard earlier,” said Grace. “After we left, Mother Cat must have pulled a sheet off the line and taken it under the fence.”

“Why?” asked Edgar.

“She used it to keep her kittens cozy under this bush,” said Wallace.

“The sheet looked like a floating ghost in the dark,” said Grace.

“And the kittens mewing was the spooky noise,” said Wallace.

Edgar tilted his head. “Then where is Mother Cat?” he asked.

“Let’s find her. We can follow her paw prints,” said Wallace. Mother Cat’s prints led out of the garden.

“What about the kittens?” asked Grace. “They are too little to leave here.”

“I have an idea!” cried Edgar. He hopped across the garden and came back with a basket. Three gardening gloves lay inside. Edgar tucked each kitten into a glove.

Then he lifted

the basket.

"Let's go!"

Mother Cat's

paw prints

led into the

yard.

Her paw

prints led

around a soccer ball.

Her paw prints led under a deck.

And there was Mother Cat!

"*Meow!*" she cried. "What are you doing with my babies?"

Edgar handed her the basket. "We found them all alone."

Mother Cat hugged the basket close. “I left to find food. I was so hungry.”

“Tell me about it!” said Edgar.

“I was coming back, but then I saw two owls in the garden. I got scared,” she said.

“That’s funny!” said Grace. “I was scared of you when I thought you were a ghost, but you were scared of me.”

“Hey, why wasn’t anyone scared of *me*?” asked Edgar.

“Rabbits are not scary,” said Wallace. “Just saying.”

“So the scary ghost in the garden was really a cat and her three kittens,” said Grace.

“Wallace and Grace solved the case! Thank you!” cried Edgar. He

tried to copy Grace's celebration dance. But shaking made him dizzy. He plopped onto the ground.

He hopped back up. "Can I go eat my kale now?"

"Eat away," said Wallace.

Edgar carried the basket of kittens with him back to the garden. Mother Cat went, too. She placed her kittens gently

under the bush and tucked the sheet around them.

Wallace and Grace flew back to the Old Tree. They watched Edgar munch on kale. He looked happy to share the garden with Mother Cat and her kittens.

Wallace wrote in his notebook: **NO GHOST!**

"Case closed," said Grace. She turned to Wallace.

But he wasn't on the branch.

Wallace was flying.

She flew after him.

He landed by a rock.

"I spotted this," said Wallace. He gave Grace a shiny gum wrapper. She liked shiny things.

"And I found this," said Grace. She pulled up a long, slimy earthworm. Wallace liked earthworms.

They were good at finding things.

They were detectives.

READ & BLOOM

PLANT THE LOVE OF READING!

Agnes and Clarabelle are the best of friends!

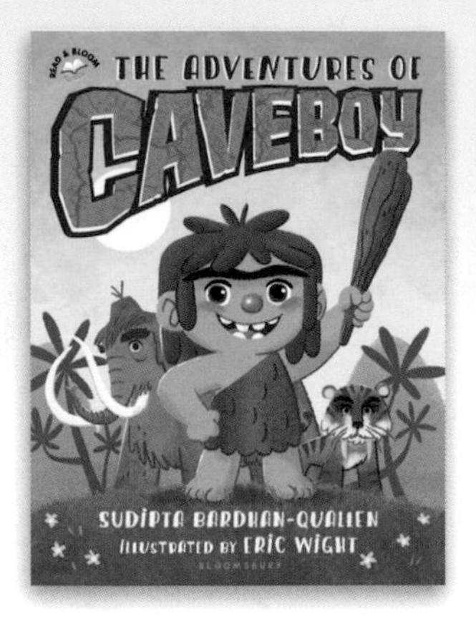

Caveboy is always ready for an adventure!

You don't want to miss these great characters! The Read & Bloom line is perfect for newly independent readers. These stories are fully illustrated and bursting with fun!

READ EVERY SERIES!

Stinky Spike can sniff his way out of any trouble!

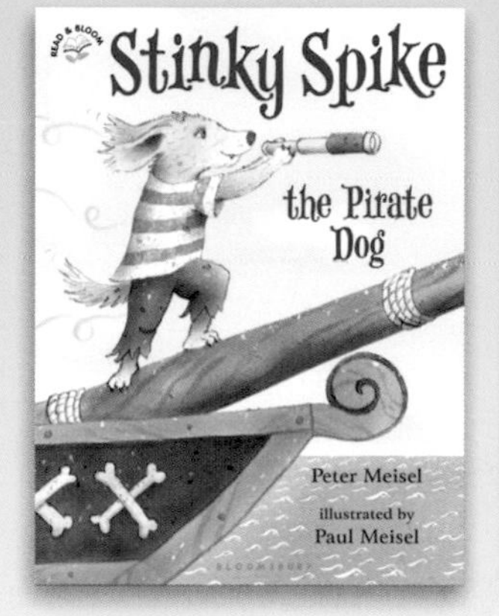

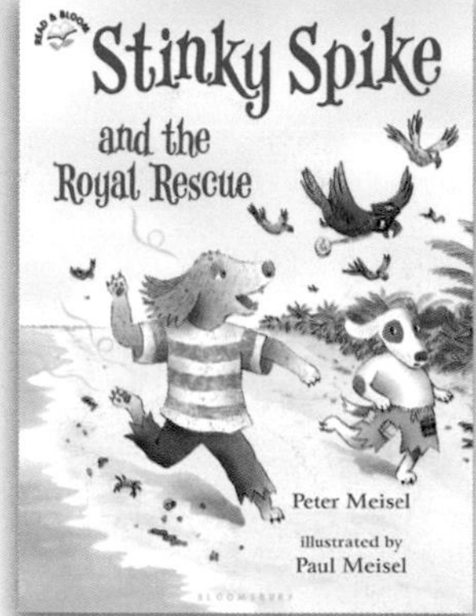

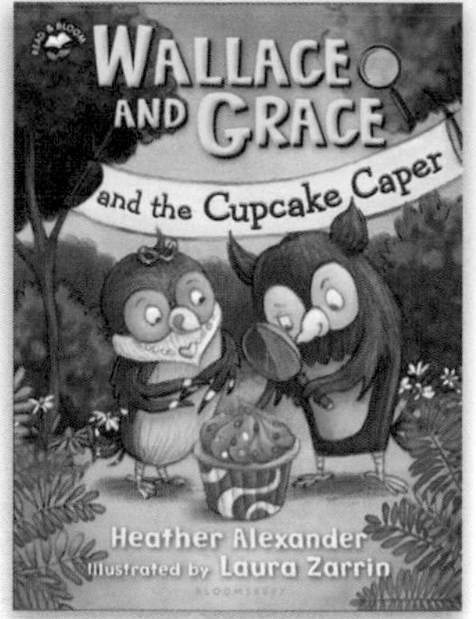

Wallace and Grace are owl detectives who solve mysteries!

Heather Alexander is the author of many books for young readers, including the Amazing Stardust Friends series. She lives by the woods in New Jersey and often finds deer, fox, turkeys, rabbits, and the occasional owl detective in her yard.

www.heatheralexanderbooks.com

Laura Zarrin is an illustrator by day and a detective by night. She is often called upon to solve mysteries for her family. She's been known to find lost shoes and lost homework and to discover who ate the last chocolate chip cookie. When she's not solving mysteries, she spends her time drawing, reading, drinking really strong iced tea, and eating fig Newtons. She lives in Northern California with her husband, their two sons, and her assistant, Cody the Chihuahua.

www.laurazarrinstudios.com